Scream Street

SKULL OF THE SKELETON

TOMMY DNBAVAND

WALKER
BOOKS

First published 2009 by Walker Books Ltd
87 Vauxhall Walk, London SE11 5HJ

4 6 8 10 9 7 5 3

Text © 2009 Tommy Donbavand
Illustrations © 2009 Cartoon Saloon Ltd

The right of Tommy Donbavand to be identified
as author of this work has been asserted by him in accordance
with the Copyright, Designs and Patents Act 1988

This book has been typeset in Bembo Educational

Printed and bound in Great Britain by Clays Ltd, St Ives plc

British Library Cataloguing in Publication Data: a catalogue record
for this book is available from the British Library

ISBN 978-1-4063-1428-1

www.walker.co.uk

For Penny, my top London agent,
without whom none of this would have happened

With special thanks to everyone at Walker Books
– especially Emma, Gill and Patrick –
who make writing Scream Street a joy

Meet the residents...

Luke Watson

Cleo Farr

Resus Negative

Dixon

Sir Otto Sneer

Samuel Skipstone

Alston and Bella Negative

Eefa Everwell

Doug

Dr Skully

Niles Farr

Mr and Mrs Watson

Who lives where...

A Sheer Hall

B Central square

C Everwell's Emporium

D No. 2: The Crudlegs

E No. 5: The Movers

F No. 11: Twinkle

G No. 13: Luke Watson

H No. 14: Resus Negative

I No. 21: Eefa Everwell

J No. 22: Cleo Farr

K No. 26: The Headless Horseman

L No. 27: Femur Ribs

M No. 28: Doug, Turf and Berry

N No. 32: Fool Spectre

O No. 39: The Skullys

Previously on Scream Street...

Luke Watson was a perfectly ordinary boy until his tenth birthday, when he transformed into a werewolf. After it happened twice more, Luke and his family were forcibly moved by G.H.O.U.L. (Government Housing Of Unusual Life-forms) to Scream Street, a community of ghosts, monsters, zombies and more.

Luke quickly found his feet, making friends with Cleo Farr (a tomboy mummy) and Resus Negative, the son of the vampires next door. Luke soon realized, however, that Mr and Mrs Watson would never get over their fear of their nightmarish neighbours. With the help of an ancient book, *Skipstone's Tales of Scream Street*, he set out to find six relics, each left behind by one of the community's founding fathers. Only their combined power will enable him to open a doorway out of Scream Street and take his parents home.

With four relics already in his possession, Luke has just two more to find. The quest for the first of these, however, will introduce he, Resus and Cleo to Scream Street's very own celebrity skeleton...

Chapter One
The Screams

The witch sprinkled a handful of dried spider-web into her cauldron and stirred. The flakes of gossamer glittered in the light of the deep orange sunset that crept in through the window.

11

Dipping a ladle into the swirling mixture, she lifted the potion to her face and inhaled deeply. Suddenly, her nostrils began to twitch and, with a huge sneeze, her nose flew across the room.

"This is never going to work!" complained the small Egyptian mummy as she rubbed at the spot where glue had held the false nose onto her bandages. "This thing just irritates me. And the robes itch, too!"

Luke Watson paused his computer game. "Yes, Cleo, so you keep saying. We'll see if we can get away without the nose." He slotted the wireless gamepad back into its charger and turned to the young vampire sitting next to him. "How are you getting on?"

"You really want me to wear my cape inside out?" asked Resus Negative.

"Yes," replied Luke, "so that the blue lining is showing." He took a short, thin piece of wood from a nearby box and handed it to Resus.

"What's this?" asked the vampire, tucking his own game controller into his cloak.

"It's a magic wand," explained Luke.

"No, it's not," said Resus. "It's a stick. Magic wands are smooth, and they have a star on top.

Like Twinkle the fairy's."

"Just *pretend* it's a magic wand, OK?" groaned Luke. "And why haven't you got the glasses on?"

Resus held up a pair of small, round spectacles. "I still don't understand why a wizard wouldn't just fix his eyesight with a simple spell."

"Incredible!" cried Luke, standing up to pull on his own costume, a black jumpsuit painted with a luminous skeleton pattern. "I spend years trick-or-treating in a bin liner cape. Then, when I finally meet a real vampire, he manages to suck all the fun out of Halloween!"

"You used to dress up as a vampire?" asked Resus incredulously.

Luke nodded. "I even used to dye my hair. It was really hard keeping the plastic fangs in as I went from door to—"

Resus strode to the window and stared moodily out into the night.

"What's the matter?" asked Luke.

Cleo punched his arm and spoke through clenched teeth. "Pretending to be a vampire? Fake fangs? Ring any bells?"

Luke's expression fell. Since arriving in Scream

13

Street he'd learnt that Resus was unusual: a normal child born to vampire parents. He wore false fangs and dyed his hair black to create the illusion that he was the same as the rest of his family, but it was still a sore point.

"Sorry," said Luke. "I suppose I don't think of you as a normal *or* as a vampire any more. You're just my friend." Resus remained silent.

"If it's any consolation," Luke continued, "I went as a mummy one year by wrapping myself in toilet paper. It poured with rain and I practically melted!"

Resus turned, beginning to smile. "I bet you were still more graceful than bumble-bandages here."

"How rude!" exclaimed Cleo, pulling the green witch's wig from her head. Snatching up the bubbling pot of liquid, she added, "I might just keep my world-famous lime tea all to myself now!"

Resus pulled a face. "It's got powdered spiderweb in. What makes you think I wanted any to begin with?"

"Right!" interrupted Luke, grabbing a pair of broomsticks from beside the door. "Take these, and then we're ready to go."

"What are they for?" asked Cleo.

"You don't want us to sweep up as we go, do you?" asked Resus.

"No," said Luke patiently, "you fly on them. Or, at least, you pretend to."

Resus and Cleo shared a glance, trying to contain their giggles. "They think witches and wizards fly about on *cleaning* tools in your world?"

Cleo clamped a broomstick between her legs and raced around the room. "Look at me," she shouted. "I'm a flying witch!" Resus fell onto the bed, laughing.

Luke pulled the skeleton mask down over his face to hide his annoyance. Who would ever have thought that Halloween could be such hard work?

Luke marched determinedly along Scream Street in his skeleton costume. Trudging miserably behind were Cleo and Resus, still dressed as witch and wizard.

"I look stupid," grunted the mummy.

"You're *supposed* to look stupid!" insisted Luke. "It's what Halloween's for."

Resus sighed. "All right, let's get this over with."

 15

"That's the spirit!"

Suddenly, a sickly green figure lurched out onto the street from a nearby garden, muttering to himself. "This is totally bogus, man! The groove has gone!"

"What's the matter, Doug?" asked Cleo, recognizing one of Scream Street's resident zombies.

Doug slouched in their direction. "I'm deep in a bad scene, little dudes."

Luke blinked at the creature's vile breath as it filtered through his skeleton mask. "Why, what's wrong?"

"I had a heavy night with Turf," explained Doug, "so I settled down for a nap in the bushes. When I woke up, just now, I found this…" The zombie turned to reveal that one of his arms was completely missing. Maggots crawled over the pus-filled shoulder. Cleo gagged.

Resus grinned at her. "What's up with you?" he asked. "I always knew Doug was *'armless*!"

Luke pulled off his mask to get a better look at the wound. It appeared that the limb had simply been torn away, leaving the decaying muscle and crumbling bone exposed. "This happened while you were asleep?" he asked, unconvinced.

Doug nodded. "Turf got hold of some brain fluid from a South American mathematician. You'll sleep through anything after a few pints of that stuff!"

"That's *handy*," quipped Resus.

Cleo elbowed the vampire and smiled at Doug sympathetically. "Who do you think took it?"

"Yeah," added Resus. "Who should *shoulder* the blame?"

The zombie shrugged – which wasn't easy to do with an arm missing.

"Do you need us to help you find your arm?" asked Resus, hoping to get out of Luke's Halloween plans.

"No thanks, little vampire dude – you're all dressed up and I'd hate for you to mess up those fine-looking duds!" The zombie gave everyone a mournful high-five with his remaining hand and shuffled away down the street.

Luke pulled his mask back on and turned to Resus and Cleo. "Right," he said. "Follow me!"

The trio wandered along the street while Luke chose his first target. The tall, misshapen houses met the dark grey clouds that swept across the moon. Dead trees burst from the pavement like hands clawing out of a grave.

Luke's family had been moved to Scream Street by G.H.O.U.L. – Government Housing Of Unusual Life-forms – after he had transformed into a werewolf and attacked a bully at his old school. Life since then had been a seemingly endless quest to locate the relics of the community's founding fathers to give Luke the power to open a doorway home and finally take his terrified parents back to their own world. Scream Street's landlord, Sir Otto Sneer, also wanted the relics for his own purposes – and in fighting to acquire them at every opportunity had turned the quest into a running battle.

Tonight, however, was going to be different. For once, Luke was determined that the search for a way out of Scream Street wouldn't be foremost in his mind. Tonight, he was going to have some fun.

"Here we are," he smiled as he led the way up the path to number 2 and rapped on the door. "Watch the master at work…"

After a moment, a huge, pulsating mass of mud and slime appeared, sipping from a crystal goblet. Clumps of muck ran down the glass.

"Ugh, children!" gurgled the bog monster. "What do you beasts want?"

"Trick or treat, Mr Crudley!" cried Luke.

Mr Crudley took another sip of wine, leaving behind tendrils of green weed. "Trick or what?"

Luke sighed. What *was* it with these people? "Trick or *treat*," he repeated.

"And what does that mean, boy?"

Luke stared up into what he hoped were the bog monster's eyes. "You have to give us a treat, like a few sweets, or we play a trick on you."

"Who is it?" called a voice from inside the house.

"It's that werewolf child," Mr Crudley called back over his shoulder. "He says he's going to play a trick on us."

Mrs Crudley, another pulsating mound of brown gloop, slithered into view beside her husband. "And why would you do that, young man?"

"Actually, I've been meaning to ask you the same thing," admitted Resus. "Halloween is the most romantic night of the year. Why do you want to go around playing tricks on people?"

Luke ripped off his skeleton mask in horror. *"Romantic?"* he asked. "Halloween isn't supposed to be romantic! It's full of monsters!"

"Exactly," gurgled Mr Crudley, wrapping a slug-like arm around his wife and nibbling affectionately at a lump of soil on her cheek. "It works for me!"

Luke was flabbergasted. "But what about Valentine's Day?"

Cleo shuddered. "Giving each other hearts? Creeps me right out! From there, you're only a short step from handing out livers, and then you're in zombie territory."

"I don't believe this," said Luke. "Halloween shouldn't be all romantic and lovey-dovey! It should be scary, and terrifying, and—"

His words were interrupted by a chorus of screams that pierced the night, causing Mr Crudley to jump and spill wine down his vast, blubbery stomach.

Luke grinned. "It should be like *that*!"

Chapter Two
The Smell

Luke, Resus and Cleo raced towards the sound, which seemed to come from the direction of Scream Street's central square. As the noise became louder, they could hear joyful cheers and screeches that seemed to be centred around one house in particular, off the opposite side of the square.

"Come on," called Luke. "Sounds like the party's this way!"

The trio skidded to a halt outside 26 Scream Street, where dozens of excited women were crowded. Female ghosts, ogres, fairies and more pressed up against the garden fence, their screeches echoing off the nearby houses.

"What's going on?" Resus asked as he, Luke and Cleo squeezed their way through the group to a gap at the front.

"He's moved in!" giggled a trembling skeleton who stood beside them. "I thought it was just a rumour, but it's not. He's actually moved to Scream Street – on Halloween, too!"

"What are you talking about?" asked Cleo. "*Who's* moved to—"

The rest of her sentence was drowned out as the front door opened and the crowd went crazy.

The trio watched as a huge, jet-black stallion leapt from the house and landed on the garden path, its hooves raising sparks from the concrete. A tall figure in a long coat was riding it: a figure with a smooth white skull for a head, sporting twisted brown horns and sharp red fangs.

The crowd screamed again as the figure winked a piercing blue eye. A female troll fainted to the ground, landing with a deafening

25

thud, and was slowly dragged away by twenty-two of her friends.

Luke nudged Cleo as the dashing rider trotted around the small front garden, waving to the hysterical crowd. "Who *is* that?"

"I've only seen him in pictures," replied Cleo, "but I think it's the Headless Horseman."

Luke looked surprised. "Unless my eyes deceive me, that guy's definitely got a head!"

"It was cut off in some battle or other," Cleo explained, "but he found it and discovered he can now take it off and on whenever he wants."

"It can't be him," scoffed Resus. "The Headless Horseman is human. This guy's got fangs and horns!"

"So he's had a little work done," barked a gravelly voice. "Anyone who's anyone has ecto-plastic surgery these days." Luke looked down to find a small, grey gargoyle standing next to him. The creature twitched a pair of granite wings on his back and held out a tiny hand. "The name's Rocky. I'm the Horseman's agent."

Luke shook the small hand, which was stone cold. "You mean his horns and fangs are fake?"

Rocky nodded. "Eddie wanted to stand out at public appearances."

"Eddie?" asked Cleo.

"The Headless Horseman's real name," replied the gargoyle impatiently. "Don't you read his fan magazine?" Cleo was about to admit that she didn't even know the Horseman *had* a fan magazine, when the celebrity himself spoke up.

"Ladies…" he began. "Now I know who put the scream in Scream Street!" The crowd squealed with delight at the sound of the Horseman's voice, reaching out to try to brush their fingertips against his leather coat as he rode past. "It's good to be back home!"

"*Back* home?" asked Resus. "But I thought…"

"Oh yes," said Rocky. "Eddie used to live in Scream Street before he was famous. Someone must have leaked the news that he was moving back."

"Now, I know you're the most loyal of fans," continued the Horseman as he circled the garden. "I expect you all bought my keep-fit video and charity CD. Many of you will have even switched

to my own brand of toothpaste. But here's the best offer of all…" The Horseman paused for every female in the crowd to hold her breath in anticipation. "Who would like to take me home with them?"

The troll fainted for a second time, flattening two banshees and a tree nymph as the street echoed with squeals of excitement once more. Rocky tugged at Luke's skeleton costume. "Good with a crowd, isn't he!"

The Horseman waited until the noise had died down enough for him to continue. "Of course, I can't actually come home with each and every one of you …"

"That's it," muttered Rocky, "build them up, then go in for the kill!"

The Horseman pulled from his pocket a glass vial, its stopper a miniature replica of his own skull. He held it out. "…but if you close your eyes, it will smell like I'm really there." He trotted along the length of the garden fence, pressing down on one of the horns on the tiny skull and spraying a fine mist over his adoring fans. "I give you my new scent!" he announced proudly. "An aromatic way to remember me – Decapitation Pour L'Homme!"

The women swooned as they breathed it in. "It smells like his leather coat," sighed a ghost.

"It smells like his riding boots," cooed a zombie.

"It smells like goblin farts!" mocked Resus, holding his nose.

Rocky glared up at the vampire. *"Shh!"* he hissed. "Don't give away the secret ingredient!"

"This scent," proclaimed Eddie to his enraptured audience, "is the first I ever smelt after my head was violently detached from my body in the heat of battle!"

The trembling skeleton beside Cleo gasped. "This is it!" she whispered. "This story is why I love him so much!"

"As those who have read my authorized

biography (available for seventeen pounds ninety-nine at all good bookstores) will know, I was asked by G.H.O.U.L. to protect an orphanage against a horde of terrifying giants." All down the street, female eyes began to mist over. "I fought valiantly for those innocent little children until the bloodthirsty leader of the giants sliced my head from my body with his sword!" The Horseman's eyes grew wet as he spoke.

"Extra tear ducts," grinned Rocky. "My idea, those."

"As my life ebbed away, all I could think of was those darling cherubs," continued the Horseman. "I couldn't die and abandon the orphans to those snarling monsters. And so, defying death itself, I picked up my severed head and continued to fight!" He paused to spray more of the perfume over the crowd.

"As the last giant fell to my blade, this is what I smelt in the air. This is the scent of courage. This is the scent of passion..." Eddie paused theatrically, then raised his horse up onto its back legs. "This is the scent of *freedom*!"

Rapturous applause and piercing screams erupted from the crowd. Rocky pushed his way

to the front and leapt over the garden gate. "OK, ladies," he shouted as he dragged cases of the perfume-filled vials from under the hedge, "first come, first served! Get your bottle of Decapitation Pour L'Homme for just twenty-nine pounds ninety-nine and you too will smell like your head-free hero!"

"This is crazy," said Luke as the crowd surged forward, producing handfuls of money from pockets and purses.

"I wouldn't be surprised if Rocky had leaked details of the Horseman's new address, just so he could sell that stinking stuff," said Resus. "It reeks!"

"It doesn't matter what it smells like," said Cleo. "He's a handsome, charming hero. He could sell anything to this lot right now."

Luke smirked. "Don't tell me you're after a bottle of the stuff too!"

"Of course not," said Cleo scornfully, "but I might get my picture taken with him when the crowd has died down." She gestured towards a slim banshee with red dreadlocks who was approaching Eddie and Rocky, a camera slung around her neck.

"Picture for *The Terror Times*?" the photographer asked.

"Always happy to oblige the press," crooned the Horseman as he wrapped his arm around the trembling skeleton, who was now at the front of the queue. "Smile!"

The photographer raised her camera and pressed the button. A dazzling burst of white light filled the street, forcing everyone to shield their eyes. As the glare of the flash faded, a single, piercing scream rang out.

The Headless Horseman's head was gone.

Chapter Three
The Relic

"**This is ridiculous!**" barked Rocky as he paced around Everwell's Emporium, the shop that stood in Scream Street's central square. The still-headless figure of the Horseman staggered around behind him. "Why isn't it working yet?"

"It's not my fault!" protested the shop's owner, Eefa Everwell. The witch lit a candle with a blue spark from her fingers, then waved her hands over a large crystal ball that was filled with hissing static. "The flash knocked everything out."

In the chaos after the disappearance of the Horseman's head, Resus had told Rocky about the recording spells Eefa used to protect her shop and suggested that they might have picked something up. Eddie's house was on the edge of square, after all. Once the disappointed crowd had dispersed, Luke, Resus and Cleo had led Rocky and his headless client to the store, where, despite protestations from the gargoyle, Eefa had allowed them to stay.

It turned out that although the spells should have captured everything, unfortunately the huge camera flash used by the newspaper photographer had prevented them from working. Eefa thought the flash must have been magical and was now working to restore the image inside the crystal ball, but it wasn't proving easy.

"I can't even rewind to before the head went missing," said the witch in frustration.

"Temporarily absent," Rocky quickly corrected her. "It's temporarily absent. The press would have a field day if they thought Eddie's head *was* missing!"

"But his head *is* missing," said Cleo, quickly

grabbing the Horseman's arm and turning his staggering frame away from a display of glass unicorns before he crashed into it. "It's the truth."

Rocky glared up at her. "I know that, and you know that – but no one outside this shop does!"

"Except for the dozens of screaming women you were selling perfume to, of course," suggested Resus with a smirk.

"Yes, except for the dozens of— Oh, shut up!" barked Rocky, turning away in a huff.

Cleo pulled her bandages up over her mouth to hide a smile. "Well, there's no one out there now except for that skeleton, so your secret is probably safe." She watched the skeletal figure sitting alone on the kerb, her face buried in her bony fingers. "She looks really sad. Maybe we should ask her inside?"

"No time for that," replied Rocky, his face creaking as he attempted a smile. "Your friend is back!"

Right on cue, Luke burst into the shop out of breath, and the bat tethered over the door let out a screech to announce his arrival. "Did you bring the book?" asked the gargoyle quickly.

Luke nodded and handed Eefa a silver-

 35

backed volume with a face protruding from the cover: *Skipstone's Tales of Scream Street*. "If anyone will know how to get the security spells working again, it'll be Mr Skipstone," he said. Eddie's body thumped into the wall beside him. Several dozen china plates commemorating the wedding of Skinderella and Prince Harming smashed to the floor.

"Will somebody sit that lumbering oaf down before he does any more damage?" demanded Eefa. "You'd think he'd be used to being headless by now!"

Rocky threw the witch a dirty look as he guided Eddie to a chair. "This 'lumbering oaf', as you call him, is the biggest celebrity ever to grace this backwater neighbourhood, so I'd be a little more polite if I were you!"

"It's not like he can hear me," muttered the witch under her breath.

"What did you tell our parents?" Resus asked Luke, pulling off his cape and clipping it back on the right way round.

"Just that Eefa has organized some Halloween games," Luke replied.

Eefa laid the silver book on the shop counter

and spoke to the face on the cover. "Mr Skipstone, my security spells have blown. Can you help?"

Samuel Skipstone's eyes opened and he smiled up at the witch. "Of course, my dear. Anything for one so captivating!" The author had spent his entire life researching and recording life in Scream Street. At the time of his death, he had cast a spell that merged his spirit with the pages of his book so that he could continue his work. Most recently, he had been providing clues for Luke and his friends to track down the relics of the founding fathers.

"There is possibly one way to restart the recording spell," began the author, opening up to reveal a page displaying a complex diagram of magical symbols. As Eefa began to study them, Rocky dragged a box over to the counter and hopped up to join her.

Cleo turned back to the shop window. The skeleton was still sitting alone outside, sobbing quietly. "I can't just leave her there," said the mummy.

"I don't think Rocky would be too pleased if you invited her in," replied Resus. "He doesn't want news of the disappearance of the Horseman's head to leak out."

"She was having her photo taken with Eddie

when it happened," snapped Cleo. "If anyone knows about it already, it's her!"

"I'm not sure…"

Cleo glanced at the gargoyle, busy discussing Skipstone's spell with Eefa at the other end of the shop. "Besides, I don't care what that lump of stone thinks," she said. "Help me open the door quietly."

With an exaggerated sigh, Resus pulled a long broom handle, a length of string and a

banana from inside his cloak. He quickly peeled the banana and tied it to the end of the pole. Raising it up to the same level as the bat, he whispered to Cleo over his shoulder, "You've got about thirty seconds!"

Luke opened the shop door as quietly as he could, and Cleo stepped outside. The bat, busy with the banana, remained silent.

"Hey!" Cleo called quietly. The skeleton raised her head. "It's OK," said the mummy. "I'm a friend. Why don't you come inside?"

"Oh no," began the nervous figure, jumping to her feet. "I couldn't…"

"Please," said Cleo. "I don't like to see you cry." Reluctantly, the skeleton followed her back into the emporium, where Luke closed the door silently behind them as Resus fed the last of the banana to the bat. Then the trio led the skeleton to a spot behind a shelving unit, where Rocky wouldn't see them if he looked up.

"What's your name?" asked Luke kindly.

"Femur," sniffed the skeleton. "Femur Ribs."

"Are you new to Scream Street?" asked Cleo. "I haven't seen you before."

Femur shook her head. "I've lived at number

39

twenty-seven for ages, but I keep myself to myself and usually stay inside a closet. When I heard that the Headless Horseman had moved in next door, I had to come out to see him."

"Well," grinned Resus, "there's still most of him over there if you fancy a look!" Cleo shot the vampire a warning look of her own.

"I've been in love with Eddie ever since I first read about him," continued Femur. "What he did to save those orphans was amazing!"

"Yeah," Resus agreed. "Anyone else in that situation could have really lost their head!" This time he got Cleo's elbow in the ribs.

"Then, when I finally meet the man of my dreams, his head disappears while I'm having my picture taken with him," moaned the skeleton.

"Which means it could well have been you who took it!" barked a voice. The trio spun round to discover Rocky standing behind them, glaring at the skeleton. "Come on," ordered the gargoyle. "You've had your fun! Hand it over." Femur dissolved into tears again.

"Don't be cruel," said Luke, defending her. "Can't you see she's upset?"

"Nothing more than crocodile tears to

throw us off the scent, I don't doubt," declared Rocky.

"I doubt even cutting off our own noses could throw us off the scent of your pongy perfume!" quipped Resus.

The gargoyle ignored him. "She must return the head that she stole!" he insisted.

"Are you insane?" demanded Cleo. "Why would she have stolen Eddie's head?"

"You'd be amazed at the lengths these stalkers go to in order to win some souvenir of their hero," retorted Rocky.

"Stalkers?" said Luke. "How can she be a stalker if she's only just left her closet, for the first time in years, to buy a bottle of your rotten perfume?"

Rocky grabbed the skeleton roughly and dragged her into the main part of the shop. "That still doesn't change the fact that this person was having her picture taken with Eddie at the time of the tragedy, that she has confessed to a lengthy obsession with him, and that no one has ever seen her before today!"

"I have," declared Samuel Skipstone from the cover of his book. "Hello, Femur."

Chapter Four
The Laboratory

"Samuel!" gasped Femur, staring at the silver-backed book in amazement. "Is it really you?"

"It is indeed," replied Skipstone. "I did not think we would ever meet again."

"So, if you two are friends," said Resus, "you must be able to vouch for her."

"I most definitely can," smiled Skipstone. "I am quite sure that Femur is innocent."

"There!" said Cleo, sticking her tongue out at Rocky. The gargoyle turned away and ruffled his granite wings sulkily.

"Thanks for your help, Mr Skipstone," said Luke.

"It is a pleasure," the author replied, "and I might be able to offer further assistance – to you this time, Luke."

"You mean…?"

"In the light of our present situation, yes, I feel I should reveal the clue to the next relic's location," said Skipstone as Luke signalled for Resus and Cleo to join him. The book flicked through its pages, stopping at an article on how to make your own coffin from a cardboard box, a roll of tape and some drinking straws.

The trio watched as the writing faded away to reveal a portion of hidden text below:

Lacking skin or muscle tone,
shining bright in bleached-white bone.
Stay ahead upon this quest
and find a skull unlike the rest

There was a pause. Then Luke spoke, his words tumbling over themselves in his excitement. "The next relic is the Headless Horseman's skull!" he breathed as the face on the book's cover closed its eyes and fell silent.

"What makes you so sure?" asked Cleo.

"Mr Skipstone said that our current situation led him to reveal the clue," explained Luke. "Why else would he tell us this on the very same day that the Headless Horseman moves back to Scream Street?"

Resus nodded. "Rocky said that Eddie used to live here ages ago," he said thoughtfully. "Although I'd never have imagined he was one of the founding fathers!"

"And *a skull unlike the rest*. There's only one person that could refer to," added Cleo.

"That's putting it mildly," laughed Resus. "He's had so much work done—"

Their conversation was interrupted by Eefa. "The spell's working again!" she exclaimed.

Everyone crowded around the crystal ball to watch the disappearance of the Horseman's head. "The picture's still a little grainy, and there's no sound," explained Eefa, "but we might be able to see what happened."

Inside the sphere, a tiny Femur stepped up next to Eddie to have her picture taken. "There! I told you she was involved!" growled Rocky.

Luke jerked his leg out and kicked the box the gargoyle stood on, sending him tumbling to the floor. "Oops!"

The blinding flash from the photographer's camera filled the crystal ball. "Keep watching," said Eefa. "We might be able to spot something as the flash dies away…"

Everyone craned their necks to get a little closer to the globe, but there was nothing to see. The Horseman's head was gone, the crowd was in shock and the banshee photographer was hurrying away, her potbelly wobbling.

"Wait a minute," said Cleo. "I don't remember the photographer having a stomach like that…"

"She didn't!" cried Luke. "I'll bet that's the Horseman's head stuffed under her shirt! The question remains, who *is* she?"

Within seconds, the disappearing thief began to change, her skin stretching and the thick dreadlocks becoming strands of long, greasy hair.

"That," announced Resus with a grin, "is

none other than our favourite landlord's shape-shifting nephew, Dixon!"

"What would *Dixon* want with the Horseman's head?" whispered Cleo as she, Luke and Resus crept along the outer wall of Sneer Hall, home to Sir Otto Sneer, first thing the following morning.

"I doubt he wants it for himself," replied Resus. "He's likely to just be the messenger boy for his uncle."

"That's what bothers me," said Luke. "How

did Sir Otto come to know that the skull was one of the relics before we did?"

"Perhaps Dixon was in the crowd outside the Horseman's house and he heard Rocky say he'd lived here before," suggested Cleo. "He might have put two and two together and worked out that Eddie was one of the founding fathers."

"That doesn't sound like the Dixon I know," said Resus. "He has trouble putting two and two together, full stop!"

"Resus is right," said Luke. "And if that was the case, how would Sir Otto have known it was the *skull* we needed? Somehow he must have worked out a way to discover which relic comes next."

"And the answer to how he did that," said Resus as the trio slipped through the wrought-iron gates and down the path to the house, "must be somewhere inside Sneer Hall." They stopped at a low window and Luke pressed his ear to the window pane. "Hear anything?" asked Resus.

"No," said Luke, "but then maybe I'm not listening hard enough…" Closing his eyes, he tried to bring on the anger that would trigger his were-wolf transformation. He thought of his parents, terrified by the unusual neighbours they now lived

among. In his mind's eye, he saw his dad, trembling as he came face to face with a vampire for the first time, and his mum, her arm broken during a vicious poltergeist attack. Slowly, the fury began to build inside him, and he forced it out.

Since he had arrived in Scream Street, Luke had begun to experience partial transformations, where only one area of his body would change. Day by day, he was learning to control these transformations, to use them in his quest to find a way home for his parents.

This time, his head was the target. His skin twisted and bones stretched to form a snout. His ears rose to the top of his scalp and lengthened, and his entire face sprouted thick, brown fur. Pressing a sensitive werewolf's ear to the window, Luke listened for a moment.

"Can you tell which room they're in?" asked Cleo.

Luke shook his head, his long whiskers quivering. "I can't hear any shoundsh," he slathered, his fangs making speech difficult, "but shomething shmellsh rotten!"

"Don't tell me," grinned Resus. "Goblin farts!" Luke nodded.

"Of course, Eddie was wearing his own scent!" said Cleo.

"And super-snout here can lead us right to him," added Resus.

Luke followed the scent around the corner of the mansion to a small side door, which to their delight they found unlocked. Soon the trio were inside Sneer Hall, walking softly along a richly decorated corridor.

"Sir Otto won't be happy if he catches us here," warned Cleo.

"We'll be in and out before he even knows it," said Resus confidently.

"That shmell'sh getting shtronger by the shecond!" interrupted Luke.

They stopped and looked around them. "There's a light coming from under that door," said Cleo, pointing further along the corridor.

"Come on," said Resus. "As quietly as we can."

"Ready?" whispered Luke, hand on the door knob.

Resus and Cleo nodded. "Ready!"

Luke slowly pushed open the door to reveal a noisy laboratory. Bottles and jars covered every

available surface, and potions of all colours whizzed through clear tubes that ran the length of the room.

The trio crept in and hid in a small space behind a pile of crates labelled *Oddbods*. "Eddie's head is definitely in here," whispered Cleo. "I can smell that awful perfume!"

"Look!" hissed Luke.

Sir Otto Sneer and his nephew, Dixon, were working at a vast, chrome table at the other end of the room. They wore surgical gowns and masks.

Luke crept along the wall behind the crates and gestured for Resus and Cleo to follow. They stayed low, taking care to keep out of Sir Otto's line of sight, and hid beneath a table, where Luke's transformation began to reverse.

"What are they doing?" mouthed Resus.

"I don't know," whispered Cleo. "But this feels more like an operating theatre than—"

Suddenly, a limp arm dangled over the side of the table, its diseased hand twitching. The mummy squealed.

Sir Otto's head jerked up and his eyes scanned the room, stopping at his nephew. "What did you scream for?"

"What?" grunted Dixon. "I didn't—"

"Just stay quiet!" snapped the landlord. "I'm trying to concentrate."

Breathing a sigh of relief, Resus squinted at the arm that now hung down over the edge of the chrome table. "That looks like the one Doug had stolen last night," he said quietly.

"There are all sorts of body parts up there," Luke whispered, paling. "And Sir Otto is stitching them together!"

Resus and Cleo leant in to see the reflection for themselves. A centaur's legs were stitched onto the huge torso of an ogre and, on the opposite side to Doug's limb, a powerful minotaur arm jutted from the shoulder. At the top of the creature, Sir Otto was busy attaching wires from the ogre's neck into Eddie's skull. Finally, he pressed down the stolen head, gluing it in place.

"There!" growled the landlord, as he stood back and tore off the mask. "Dixon – throw the switch!"

His scrawny nephew giggled and pulled on a lever that sent sparks of fizzing blue electricity streaming through the monster. The energy buzzed between Eddie's fake horns, and the creature sat bolt upright with a roar.

Sir Otto laughed madly, his eyes lit up by the flashing bursts of power. "I've done it, Dixon!" he yelled. "IT'S ALIVE!"

Chapter Five
The Demon

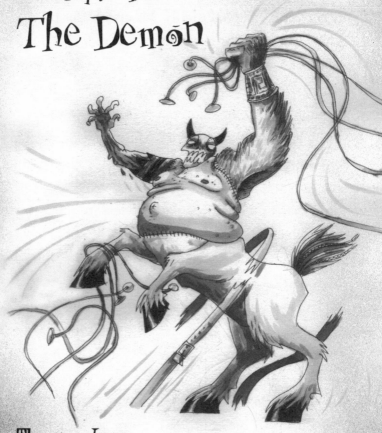

The creature arched its back as the electricity surged through its body, roaring so loudly that Luke, Resus and Cleo were forced to cover their ears.

The monster's minotaur arm flexed against its restraint, snapping the leather strap that secured

it to the table. Leaping to its hooves, the beast tore away the sensors from its chest as a final burst of power settled around its neck, forming an electrical collar. The creature growled and turned to face the landlord, staring down at him through pulsing green eyes.

"I-I am your creator," stuttered Sir Otto nervously. "You will do my bidding." The monster raised its clenched fists into the air, but the landlord stood firm. "I name you Ottostein!" he proclaimed.

The creature took a step forward, causing Dixon to squeal and retreat across the room. He hid behind the crates, where he found himself face to face with Luke, Resus and Cleo. "Oh, hello," he said good-naturedly. "What are you doing here?"

"What is *that*?" demanded Luke as the creature burst out of the laboratory in hot pursuit of the trio, who were now fleeing back along the corridor.

"Well, don't quote me on this," said Resus as the monster picked up an ancient suit of armour on display and hurled it after their retreating backs. "But the only thing I know of with bright

green eyes like that is a demon!" A diamond-encrusted breastplate smashed to the ground inches behind him.

"A demon?" shouted Cleo, putting on an extra burst of speed as the side door came into view. "My uncle Ramses had bright green eyes, and he wasn't a demon!" The trio burst through the door and out into the grounds.

"Yes," agreed Resus, "but your uncle Ramses wasn't intent on tearing everyone around him into wafer-thin strips!"

The demon crashed out of the mansion and gazed around, taking in its new surroundings. Sir Otto Sneer soon appeared behind it, a thick cigar clamped between his teeth and a box covered in switches in his hands. The controls fizzed with blue power. "The fake vampire is correct," he barked. "This is indeed a demon – with one small difference …"

The landlord flicked a switch and the demon growled, flashes of electricity sparking between its horns. "…*I* control Ottostein's every move!"

"A remote-control demon," breathed Luke in amzement. "Now I've seen everything."

"You've seen *nothing* yet, boy!" bellowed Sir

Otto, his fingers deftly working the controls. The demon turned and advanced slowly upon the trio, its emerald eyes blazing. "This monster will bring Scream Street to its knees!" cackled the landlord. "It is a creature of pure malevolence and evil, intent on nothing but carnage." He wiped away a tear as his eyes grew misty. "It's like the son I never had!"

"I thought *I* was the son you never had," squeaked Dixon from behind his uncle.

The landlord grunted. "If you were the son I'd never had, I'd never have had you!" Dixon faltered, trying to work out whether or not he'd just been insulted.

Luke, Resus and Cleo backed away around a nearby tree.

As they did so, Sir Otto rotated a dial on his controller, causing the demon to rip the tree up by its roots and swing it around like a sword.

"The question that remains," rumbled the landlord as Luke ducked out of the way of the oncoming branches, "is why did you three break into my lab? You couldn't have known I was working on Ottostein…" He gazed up at the Headless Horseman's skull, his eyes widening.

"The head is one of your precious relics, isn't it!"

Luke's breath caught in his chest. So Sir Otto *hadn't* known that Eddie was one of the founding fathers! "N-no, of course not," he lied.

"You can't fool me, boy," grinned Sir Otto, biting down on his cigar. "I've been collecting body parts for months – then, joy of joys, G.H.O.U.L. tells me that the Headless Horseman is moving in. All I needed was his head to complete my creation – but, what do you know, I get one of the magical relics into the bargain!"

Triumphantly, the landlord pressed another button and the trio ducked as Ottostein finally threw the tree at them, barely missing Cleo. While Sir Otto looked on, laughing gleefully, Luke, Resus and Cleo ran.

Luke gazed miserably out of the window of the emporium. "This is all my fault," he sighed.

The group had spent a long, restless night inside the shop and, as dawn broke, there seemed to be no chance of escape. Outside, Ottostein battered its monstrous fists against the shield spell Eefa had placed around the building. Rocky paced nervously across the shop floor.

"How is it your fault?" asked Resus.

"Sir Otto had no idea the skull was one of the relics," replied Luke. "We gave that away by breaking in to get it back."

"Then if anything it's 'our' fault," said Resus. "We're in this together, remember."

Luke smiled gratefully at his friend, then turned to Eefa, who sat cross-legged on the counter, her eyes closed in concentration as she kept the shield spell in place. "How are you holding out?"

"We're safe," said the witch. "For now." She aimed a finger at a nearby candle to ignite its wick. "We'll have to find a more permanent solution soon, though." Outside the shimmering purple haze of the spell, Dixon clapped excitedly as Sir Otto ordered the demon to increase its attack.

"Poor Eddie," groaned Femur as she gazed through the window at the Horseman's burning eyes. "What are they doing to you?" The Horseman's body remained rigid in a chair behind her.

"What I'd like to know," said Cleo, "is where they got those body parts from. I know that's Doug's missing arm, but what about the others?"

"There were a lot of crates in there with

'Oddbods' written on the side," said Resus thoughtfully.

Rocky stopped his pacing. "Oddbods?" he said. "That's where I got Eddie's extra parts from: his horns, fangs and tear ducts."

"You can *buy* body parts from that place?" demanded Luke.

Rocky nodded. "Quality stuff. Whatever parts Sneer used, they'll be from the strongest and toughest of their species. I wouldn't be surprised if that demon is virtually unstoppable."

Tired of watching Ottostein batter fruitlessly against the magical shield around the shop, Sir Otto pressed a series of buttons on his remote control and forced the creature's attention away from the emporium to one of the houses that bordered the square. The monster's collar of sparking, blue electricity fizzed as the order was given.

The occupants of the store watched in horror as the demon ripped away the garden fence, then smashed a hole in the wall of the house. A family of elves came running out, screeching in terror as Ottostein lumbered through the hole and began to demolish their living room. Sir Otto roared with laughter and Dixon danced around him.

"I've had enough of this…" snapped Luke, marching towards the door.

Resus grabbed his arm. "Exactly what do you plan to do? Let it kill you over and over until it's too tired to attack anyone else?"

"I… I don't know," replied Luke. "But I have to do something. *Someone* has to do something!"

"Let *me* go out there," said Femur determinedly. "Let me try to reason with him."

Resus looked shocked "You want to go out there and try to reason with a remote-controlled demonic killing machine?"

"Not with the demon," said the skeleton firmly. "With Eddie. He's still inside that head somewhere, and I think I can reach him. If I do, then I'm sure the head can override the signals being sent to the rest of the body."

Luke, Resus and Cleo exchanged glances. "It's worth a try," said the mummy.

Femur opened the door and stepped outside. Eefa dropped the shield long enough for the trembling skeleton to pass through, and everyone else gathered at the window to watch her cross the square.

Dixon saw her first. "Uncle Otto!" he called.

Sir Otto growled, still concentrating on the controls in his hands. Ottostein was busy smashing the windows of number 36. "Sir!" thundered the landlord. "How many times have I got to tell you? It's *sir*!"

"Sorry, *Sir* Uncle Otto," simpered Dixon, "but I think you'd better look."

A smile spread across the landlord's face as he turned to see Femur approaching. "Well, well," he said, stroking the silk scarf around his throat, "we appear to have a heroine on the loose…"

And with a sharp punch of a button, he ordered the demon to stride over towards the skeleton. They met in the centre of the square.

Femur gazed up into the flashing green eyes of the monstrous creature. "Eddie," she said softly. "You've never really met me, but I've known you for so very long. I'm your number-one fan."

The green lights dimmed briefly, then Sir Otto sent another burst of electricity through the demon. The monster screamed in pain and the pulsing emeralds returned to full brightness.

"I know you don't want to be part of this," continued Femur. "I know you don't want to hurt people. So – please – come back to us and end it now."

"Bor-ring!" yelled Sir Otto, turning a dial on the remote control. Ottostein roared and grabbed Femur by the neck, lifting her off the ground.

"No!" screamed Cleo from the other side of the glass, but she could only watch as the demon hurled the skeleton across the square. Femur crashed against the wall around Sneer Hall and lay very, very still.

Chapter Six
The Rampage

Cleo burst out through the doors of the emporium and found herself blocked by the magical shield.

"Eefa, lower the spell!" shouted Luke, close behind. The witch clicked her fingers and the purple haze around the shop vanished, allowing Cleo to race across to square to Femur's side. Luke and Resus were just seconds behind her.

Cleo dropped to her knees beside the skeleton. "Please be OK…" she pleaded. Femur's eyes had

regained their focus, but they were staring past Cleo rather than at her.

"Well, what do you know?" came the voice of Sir Otto from behind the mummy. "I get to crush two freaks for the price of one!" Cleo spun round to see the demon charging towards her.

Luke leapt in front of Ottostein, placing himself between Cleo and the monster, but, with a single swipe of its fist, it knocked him to the ground and continued.

Resus pulled a long, silver sword from the folds of his cape and charged at the demon, but he too was thwarted as it snatched the weapon from his hands and snapped it like a twig. Kicking Resus aside, Ottostein stomped towards Cleo and Femur, the landlord laughing in the background.

Just as the demon reached the terrified mummy, the air behind Sir Otto began to shimmer. Suddenly, a stumpy leg appeared, followed by another, as a large, round woman dressed all in black climbed through some kind of hole in the air, dragging a huge suitcase behind her.

Luke stared in amazement. A Hex Hatch, of course! This was a window into Scream Street

that could only be opened by G.H.O.U.L. itself. He had never seen one this close before.

Pulling hard on the suitcase, the woman swung round and hit Sir Otto squarely in the back. The landlord fell to the ground, the remote control bouncing out of his hands and smashing as it hit the concrete.

Ottostein paused as the flow of electricity ceased, its hands just inches from Cleo's throat. The demon flexed its fingers, realizing that it was no longer under Sir Otto's control. Roaring with delight at this sudden freedom, the monster abandoned its task and pounded away across the square, crashing through a garden fence and disappearing down the street.

"You moron!" ranted Sir Otto, clambering to his feet and turning to see who had knocked him over. "How could you be so stu—" His eyes widened in alarm and he turned deathly pale. "Oh no," he whimpered. "Not you…"

With a squeal of excitement, Dixon raced over to the woman in black and flung his arms around her sturdy frame. "Mummy!"

"What are *you* doing here, Queenie?" Sir Otto whispered.

"Do I need an excuse to visit the family home?" bellowed the woman, smoothing a barely visible crease from her black silk dress. "It's as much my house as it is yours." She jabbed at the remains of the remote control unit with the sharp tip of a very pointed shoe. "Still playing with toys, I see, Otto."

Dixon was now bouncing excitedly around his mother. "Is Dad with you?"

Queenie Sneer shook her head. "He shapeshifted into a garden gnome about a month ago. Says he won't change back while I'm still around."

"Don't blame him," muttered Sir Otto, his courage returning.

"So, seeing as G.H.O.U.L. was already opening this Hex Hatch to allow someone to move in," continued his sister, "I have reverted to my maiden name – and come home!" She slapped Sir Otto enthusiastically around the back of the head as she spoke.

The landlord sulkily rubbed his scalp and gathered up the pieces of broken remote control. "This is ruined!" he grunted, shaking the box and listening despairingly to the rattle it made.

Meanwhile, Luke, Resus and Cleo were helping Femur to stand. "I see you've still got the freaks running around this dump," said Queenie, looking down her nose at the trembling skeleton.

"And *I* see you're about as pleasant as your brother!" retorted Cleo.

"Cleo…" warned Luke.

Queenie waddled over to face the mummy.

"You useless, bandaged nobody. How dare you speak to your elders in that manner!"

"Elders?" laughed Cleo. "I was entombed six thousand years ago – I doubt you're anywhere near as old as me!" She looked the frumpy woman up and down. "Although, if your dress sense is anything to go by—"

"OK!" interrupted Resus, grabbing Cleo's arm and quickly steering her away as Queenie flushed an angry shade of purple. "We have to be going now!"

Luke stepped up to Sir Otto. "Not until he calls off his demon."

The landlord thrust the remains of the remote control at Luke. "With what?" he demanded. "My idiot of a sister put paid to my fun!"

Queenie reached out with a black-gloved hand and pulled Sir Otto up by the ear. "I suggest you show this 'idiot' to her room before anything else painful happens to you," she hissed, dragging her brother towards Sneer Hall.

"Well," said Resus as the three Sneers disappeared from view, "if Sir Otto can't stop the demon ..."

"...then it's up to us!" finished Luke.

*   *   *

The trio followed the trail of ripped-up hedges, broken gates and shattered windows along Scream Street. There was a gaping hole in the front of number 13 where the front door should be.

"What were the chances it would choose my house?" sighed Luke as he, Resus and Cleo raced up the garden path.

Inside, the house was a scene of total destruction. Walls had been demolished, furniture smashed and floorboards torn up.

"Do you think this was the demon?" asked Cleo looking around her in horror.

"No," Luke replied sarcastically. "My mum and dad are redecorating the place in traditional monster-aftermath style!"

"Kids," came a strangled cry from above, "get out of here!"

Luke, Resus and Cleo looked up. Standing at the top of the stairs was Ottostein, electric collar fizzing around its throat, with Luke's dad in its grip. Mr Watson's feet wriggled and kicked as the monster lifted him higher into the air with its stolen zombie arm. "Just go!" he urged them,

71

barely able to get the words out.

"Put him down," ordered Luke, "or you'll regret it!"

Ottostein laughed and spoke for the first time since its creation. "Run away, child," it rumbled. "Nothing can stop my lust for anarchy, least of all you. I shall destroy you all!"

Luke froze as he saw his mum appear on the landing behind the demon, a heavy table lamp clutched in her hands.

"No!" he called to her. "Don't do it!"

Ottostein laughed, unaware of Mrs Watson behind him. "You think I will cease my rampage simply because you give the order?" He tightened his grip around Mr Watson's throat and Luke clenched his own fists as he watched his dad's face turn red, then purple.

Ignoring her son's warning, Mrs Watson raised the lamp above her head and brought it down hard on the demon's shoulder. The weapon was blunt but heavy enough to tear the crude stitches that held the arm in place. Ottostein screamed with rage as the arm fell away, releasing Luke's dad as it did so.

The demon turned and grabbed Mrs Watson

by the hair with its remaining hand, tossing her effortlessly down the stairs. Luke, Resus and Cleo dashed to her side as she crashed to the bottom.

"Mum!" shouted Luke, pulling her to the safety of the living room. "Are you OK?" A semiconscious groan was the only response.

Ottostein laughed wickedly. "You are no match for me!" it roared.

Luke felt a shadow begin to creep over his mind as he glared up at the monster. "Oh, it's not *me* you need to worry about," he replied. "It's my furry friend!" Anger flooded through Luke, this time setting off a full werewolf transformation. Sharp talons burst through the ends of his fingers and toes, muscles rippled as they repositioned themselves around his bones, and his skin flushed with coarse fur.

The werewolf howled once before racing up the stairs and launching itself at the demon, teeth bared. Ottostein lashed out with the back of its powerful minotaur arm and sent Luke crashing into the banisters, splintering the wood as he fell. But the wolf was back on its feet in seconds, running towards the demon for a second attack.

This time Luke stayed low, ducking beneath

the demon's hand and sinking his fangs deep into its leg.

The demon roared with laughter and gripped the werewolf by the scruff of its neck. "You think I worry about pain?" it bellowed, hurling Luke against the door to his bedroom.

Resus dashed up the stairs, dodging the monster's fist. He gripped his friend by the fur and spoke urgently into his ear. "Go for the head," he urged. "The stitches holding Doug's arm in place

weren't strong – if you can separate the head from the body, we might stand a chance of stopping this thing!"

The werewolf snarled in acknowledgement, saliva dripping from its fangs as it turned and leapt for Ottostein's skull. Gripping one of the horns between its teeth, the wolf flipped itself over the demon's shoulder and pulled with all its might.

The demon's head jerked back, Sir Otto's glue beginning to give at the front of its neck. Sensing danger, Ottostein slammed itself against the wall, trapping the werewolf and forcing it to release its grip.

The wolf collapsed to the floor and the demon bounded down the stairs and smashed clumsily out of the house.

"Luke!" As Resus scrambled to reach his friend, Luke's body began to ripple and he slowly changed back to human form.

"My mum…?" he breathed.

"Cleo's with her," said Resus. "She's OK, but your dad's unconscious." The vampire slumped back against the wall. "Short of building a demon of our own, I don't see how we can even come close to defeating that thing!"

A smile spread slowly across Luke's face. "That sounds suspiciously like a plan…"

Chapter Seven
The Plan

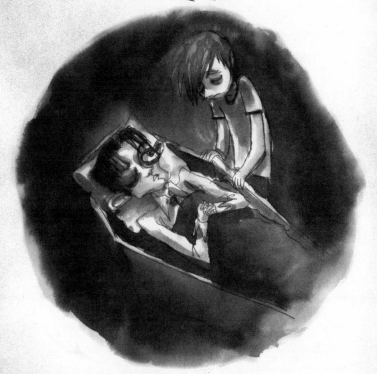

Luke gazed down at his father's pale face in the silk-lined coffin. "At least you're at rest now, Dad," he said quietly.

"I most certainly am *not* at rest!" exclaimed Mr Watson, sitting bolt upright. "And I am *not* sleeping in a coffin. I'm going home."

"There isn't much of a home to go back to – the demon destroyed almost all of it," Luke reminded his father as he climbed unsteadily to his feet. "It's good of Resus's parents to let us stay here until we tidy things up, so don't be ungrateful."

"I'm not ungrateful, Luke," said Mr Watson, clinging to the side of the coffin as a wave of dizziness came over him. "I'm scared. Your mum's scared. We tried to fight that thing, and we lost. We're not meant to be in this place. We don't belong here!"

Luke hadn't told his parents about his quest to open a doorway home; he didn't want to get their hopes up. What if he failed in the task and they remained stranded in Scream Street? He left the room, fighting back the feeling that his quest might actually be making things worse for them.

Bella Negative stepped out of the next bedroom and gave Luke a smile. "Do you want to go in and see your mum?" she asked. "She's awake."

Luke shook his head. "I'll let her rest and pop in later."

He found Resus and Cleo waiting for him outside. "What now?" asked the mummy.

Luke looked at his friends with determination on his face. "We get back into Sir Otto's lab and build ourselves a demon."

"I'll have tulips and daffodils, Otto," barked Queenie Sneer as she ambled through the gardens of Sneer Hall, "and I want them all dyed black before you put them in my room." The landlord muttered an insult under his breath before reluctantly dropping to his knees to pick the flowers.

"Oh look, Mummy!" squealed Dixon, his arm through his mother's. "Snapdragons! Snapdragons would look lovely in my bedroom."

"You heard the boy," ordered Queenie. "Pick him some snapdragons."

Sir Otto clambered to his feet and bit down hard on his cigar. "If that idiot wants snapdragons, let him get them himself," he barked defiantly.

Queenie Sneer slapped her brother across the back of the head, sending him crashing back to the ground. "*That's* for not doing what you're told ..." she snarled before kicking him hard on the bottom. Sir Otto fell forward, his face landing in the prickly thorns of a rose bush. "...and *that's* for calling my darling boy an idiot!"

Watching the scene from behind a hedge, Resus stuffed the corner of his cape into his mouth to stifle his laughter. "This is brilliant!"

"It's little enough punishment for what he's done by creating that demon," Cleo pointed out.

"It's a start, though," said Luke. "Come on, let's get into Sneer's lab while they're busy playing happy families."

Resus took one last glance behind him to see Queenie and Dixon relaxing on a double swing, ordering the sweating landlord to push them. Grinning widely, the vampire followed his friends towards Sneer Hall.

Once inside the lab, Luke closed the door behind them. "Right," he said, "we're looking for parts to build a monster."

"I've been meaning to ask you about that," said Cleo as Resus began to rummage through the Oddbods crates. "Even if we find an entire body's worth of bits, how do we assemble them?"

Luke scanned the jugs of bubbling liquid and test tubes of mysterious coloured powder that filled the room. "The answer's got to be in here somewhere," he said. "I thought you might be able to figure it out."

"Me?" demanded Cleo. "Why?"

Luke shrugged. "You're the one who brews her own herbal teas."

"There's a world of difference between inventing hot drinks and creating life itself, Luke Watson," Cleo exclaimed.

"Well, it's a darn sight closer than anything I can do," retorted Luke. "My only skills involve getting to level seven in Martial Arts Madness II and being able to turn my eyelids inside out!"

"Right," interrupted Resus as he lay a collection of body parts out on the vast chrome table. "I've got three hands, some spare fingers, a leg and a couple of bellybuttons." He leant in to peer a little closer. "At least, I *hope* they're bellybuttons…"

"Wonderful!" groaned Luke. "We can build ourselves a demon, but one that's limited to playing the piano and collecting fluff!"

"I don't see why we need all this stuff when we've got a perfectly good body sitting back at Everwell's Emporium," Cleo commented.

Luke and Resus stared at her.

"Say that again," said Luke.

"I'm simply wondering why we're scrabbling around for parts to build a demon from scratch when the Horseman's body is sitting back at Eefa's doing nothing," she said. "We just need a head for it."

"And it didn't occur to you to suggest this *before* I spent ten minutes rifling through assorted body parts?" asked Resus.

"Come on!" said Luke, grabbing the handful of loose fingers and dumping them back into one of the crates. "I know what to do."

He turned to pull open the door to the laboratory just as Sir Otto Sneer pushed it from the opposite side. There was a brief moment's silence as Luke, Resus and Cleo stared at the landlord in surprise, then Sir Otto leapt into the room and slammed the door behind him.

"Hide me!" he hissed.

"What?"

"Hide me! She's coming!"

"Who's coming?" asked Cleo.

"My insane sister," growled Sir Otto. "Who do you think?" The landlord's clothes were filthy and his face was covered with a thin veil of sweat. He dashed around the lab, opening drawers and cupboards as he searched for a place to conceal himself. "She's only been here for a few hours, and I can't take any more!"

"Oh, Otto … where are you?" Queenie Sneer's voice echoed along the corridor. With a squeal that would have made a four-year-old girl proud, Sir Otto dived under the table and lay there, quivering.

"Er… He doesn't appear to have mentioned that we've broken into his secret lab," Resus said to Luke.

"Maybe he's got other things on his mind?" suggested Cleo.

"Which puts *us* at an advantage," smiled Luke. He knelt down and peered at Sir Otto under the table. "What will you give us if we hide you from your sister?"

"Take anything you want," whispered the landlord. "Just keep her as far away from me as possible!"

"What I *want*," said Luke, "is for you to call off your demon."

"Can't be done," answered the landlord. "You saw the remote control: it was smashed. Once that happened, the connection to the demon was severed."

"So," said Cleo, "connect it up again."

"Impossible," said Sir Otto. "It has to be powered by the same batteries."

"That monster runs on batteries?" exclaimed Resus.

"Not the kind you're thinking of," replied the landlord. "Normal batteries would run down too quickly, so I powered the demon with electrically charged bats."

Cleo paled beneath her bandages. "You killed bats to make your … thing?"

"Of course not," said Sir Otto. "What use would they be to me then? I simply zapped a couple until they were fizzing a bit. When they're flapping around inside the creature's body, they generate power of their own."

"You disgust me!" exclaimed Cleo, rushing over to the door and flinging it open. "I'm going to find your sister and tell her where you're hiding."

"You already have," bellowed Queenie Sneer as she stormed along the corridor towards the laboratory. "I wondered which of these rooms Otto would be cowering in. And he appears to have found some trespassers!"

Cleo tried to close the door again and Luke and Resus dashed forward to lend their weight, but, with a single shove of her black-gloved hand, Queenie sent the trio sprawling. Bottles and jars smashed as they scurried to join Sir Otto beneath the table.

The remaining body parts fell from the table and landed in Resus's lap, including a slice of flesh sporting a jagged scar. He held it to his forehead and turned to Luke. "*Now* do I look like your precious wizard?" he asked.

Chapter Eight
The Deal

"How do you freaks suggest we get ourselves out of this?" demanded Sir Otto as he peeled what seemed like the millionth potato in a row.

"Well," said Resus, pausing in the middle of chopping a mountain of carrots, "for one, we haven't actually agreed to help you yet — and two, I'd stop calling us freaks if you want us to."

The landlord blew out a huge cloud of cigar smoke and muttered something rude but carried

on peeling. Queenie had put Luke, Resus and Sir Otto to work in the kitchens of Sneer Hall, preparing a huge banquet for the new lady of the house and her son.

Resus added another handful of chopped carrots to the pile beside him. "It shouldn't be difficult to break out," he said.

"We're not going anywhere without Cleo," said Luke firmly. After calling Queenie an overbearing sack of spanners, the mummy had been dragged away along the corridor for the insult, leaving the others to prepare the food. Queenie wanted "the little troublemaker" where she could see her.

"If we do hide you from your sister," Luke said to Sir Otto as he mixed together a huge bowl of eggs, "you have to help us build our own demon to take on yours."

"For a whole demon," said the landlord, "I'll need a more permanent solution to the Queenie problem."

"Permanent?" gasped Resus. "You don't mean…?"

"Of course not!" snarled Sir Otto. "I'm not going that far. I'm just talking about pushing her

back through the Hex Hatch and into another G.H.O.U.L. community. It doesn't matter which one – anywhere will do!"

Luke held out his hand to Sir Otto. "Deal?"

The landlord shook it. "Deal!"

"Now *that's* something I never thought I'd see," grinned Resus.

"There is, however, one small problem," said Sir Otto. "If we're going to build a fully functional demon, we'll need to get out of here."

"I've been thinking about that," said Luke. "The best time to make our move would be when we're—"

"Shh!" hissed Resus. "Someone's coming!"

The kitchen door flew open and Dixon waltzed in looking pleased with himself. "Mummy wants to make a few changes to the dinner menu," he announced. "First, there are to be only egg whites in the omelette; second, the potatoes are to have their skins left on; and third—"

Sir Otto glared at his ginger-haired nephew. "...anything resembling a carrot is to be chopped into tiny little pieces?"

Dixon swallowed hard but stood his ground. "Now, now," he gulped. "Don't make me call

Mummy in here to sort you out … Otto."

"Otto?" roared the landlord. "How dare you? It's Sir Uncle Otto – I mean, *Sir* Otto – to you!" Dixon screamed as his uncle charged through the mound of potato peelings and leapt upon him.

"I guess now would be when we're making our move, then," shouted Resus as he and Luke threw down their utensils and raced to pull Sir Otto and Dixon apart.

"I'll chew him up and spit him out!" yelled the landlord as Luke struggled to hold him back. Resus wasn't so much holding Dixon back as stopping him from running to mummy. The last thing they needed was interference from Queenie.

"Tie him up," said Resus, pulling a length of rope from his cloak. As Luke got to work, Sir Otto grabbed a handful of cutlery and began knotting forks and spoons to Dixon's lank, ginger hair.

"This way," explained the landlord, "if he shapeshifts into something slim enough to escape his bonds, we should be able to hear him coming a mile off!" Ten minutes later, Dixon's hair clanged like a wind chime whenever he moved.

"OK," said Resus. "What now?"

Luke snatched up a silver tray and began to

pile it with food. "Now," he said, "we serve up some revenge!"

"Do you know," said Queenie Sneer as she sipped at her goblet of champagne, "I've never really spent any quality time with one of you little freaks before. I think I might like to keep you."

Beside her at the dining table, Cleo sat tied to a chair with her own bandages, guarded by Sir Otto's two ravenous hellhounds.

"What a wonderful idea," the mummy replied

sarcastically. "You could keep me in a kennel and teach me to fetch a stick."

"Oh, I wouldn't go that far!" laughed Queenie, missing the edge to Cleo's words. "I'm sure there's more than enough room in the cellar for you to sleep."

"Why are you like this?" demanded Cleo. "You married one of us 'freaks'! Dixon's dad is a shapeshifter, isn't he?"

"I was young and foolish," snarled Queenie, "and naive enough to think he could shape-shift into something a little less weird once we'd moved to a more up-market G.H.O.U.L. community." She sighed. "You can take the freak out of Scream Street, but you can't take Scream Street out of the freak!"

There was a moment's silence and then Queenie frowned. "Where *is* that son of mine?" she asked no one in particular. "I only sent him to deliver a message to the kitchen staff."

"I'm afraid Dixon has been unavoidably detained," answered Luke, entering at that moment with a covered tray. "He's a little tied up," he added, winking at Cleo. Resus and Sir Otto followed, laden with plates and dishes.

Luke placed the silver tray before Queenie and lifted the lid to reveal his bowl of uncooked omelette mix.

"What's this?" the woman demanded.

"Oh, nothing serious," snarled Sir Otto from behind her. "Just a bit of a *yolk*!" And with that he grabbed his sister's head and pushed her face deep into the bowl. "We have to get rid of her now," he shouted to Luke as Queenie spluttered angrily in the raw egg, "or my life won't be worth living!"

Chaos erupted on all sides. Using a knife he'd brought from the kitchen, Resus sliced through the bandages securing Cleo to her chair, then tossed the mummy a soup ladle. Catching it, Cleo turned just as one of the hellhounds leapt for her throat. She swiftly bopped it on the head with the ladle and the dog fell down, unconscious.

Queenie lifted her face from the bowl, gasping for air. Sir Otto ducked as she wiped sticky egg yolk from her eyes and threw a heavy salt cellar in his direction. It smashed against the wall just above the landlord's head.

Luke took the opportunity to hurl a bag of flour at Queenie, which split and covered its target with fine, white powder.

"Careful," quipped Resus as he fought off the second hellhound with a loaf of bread, "she'll claim you *battered* her!"

"If you think *omelet*ting you get away with a gag like that…" said Luke.

Resus grinned, but not for long as Queenie swung at him with a bowl of tomato soup. He pulled back just in time and the hot, red liquid spilt down the front of Queenie's dress, causing her to yell.

Sir Otto roared with laughter as his sister stumbled forward and cracked her shin on the leg of the dining table. Queenie quickly retaliated, however, by grabbing two halves of an onion and grinding them into her brother's eyes.

Sir Otto screeched in pain and dropped to his knees, blinded by the onion. As he crawled in the direction of the door, his fingers came upon a shoe and, thinking it was Luke, he reached his hand up for help. "Come on!" he snapped.

"Don't make me do it!" squealed a familiar voice. Sir Otto squinted up through burning eyes to find Dixon – all his hair lopped off – holding a huge pumpkin over him.

"You haven't the guts," sneered his uncle.

"You're nothing but a wimp!"

At this, Dixon's eyes flooded with tears, and as he went to wipe them, he accidentally released the pumpkin. The massive vegetable fell, wedging fast over Sir Otto's head.

Luke slapped the second hellhound across the face with a raw fish. "This is more like the Halloween I know!" he whooped.

Suddenly terrified at what he had done, Dixon grabbed Queenie's hand and dragged her out of the room. The hellhound gave chase.

Finally free of the snarling dog, Resus jumped up onto a chair and opened one of the small, high windows. "Time to get out of here!" he yelled.

Cleo looked doubtfully up at the tiny opening. "You'll never get through there," she said.

"I don't need all of me to get out," said Resus, producing a megaphone from the folds of his cloak. "Just my voice." He turned and yelled through the window, "Oi, Ottostein – you big, ugly, do-it-yourself demon! Come and have a go if you think you're hard enough!"

Then, jumping down from the chair and grabbing Cleo's hand, Resus pulled her under the table, where the mummy was surprised to find

Luke and Sir Otto already hiding. Within seconds there was a colossal roar and Sir Otto's monstrous creation burst into the dining room. Not seeing the crouching figures beneath the table, Ottostein continued smashing his way through the house, searching for his challenger.

Resus helped Cleo to her feet, then gestured towards the gaping hole that led out to the grounds of Sneer Hall and freedom. "Your exit awaits, m'lady!"

Chapter Nine
The Rival

"That thing is destroying my beautiful home!" wailed Sir Otto Sneer, wiping tears from his eyes as he watched the carnage from the safety of Everwell's Emporium.

"Not a nice feeling, is it," said Luke. "But at least I didn't cry when it happened to me."

"I'm NOT crying!" roared Sneer. "It's those darned onions my sister rubbed in my eyes. They won't stop running!"

Eefa pulled the Horseman's body to its feet. "You're certain this will work?" she asked Luke.

"I hope so," he replied. "Sir Otto thinks he can repeat the process he used on the first demon." He took a heavy sword from its display rack on the wall and clamped the handle into the Horseman's hand. "It's got to be worth a try."

"I'm not sure I like this idea," said Rocky. "Eddie's my top client, and I need his body in perfect condition for a movie audition next week."

"Fair enough," said Resus, opening the shop door as an invitation for him to leave. "You go off and stop the demon yourself, and we'll keep Eddie's body nice and safe here."

Cleo snatched up a broom and waved it menacingly in Rocky's direction. "I'll come along later and sweep up what's left of you, shall I?" The gargoyle paled to an even lighter shade of grey and shut his mouth.

Luke turned to the trembling figure of Femur. "Are you sure you want to go through with this?" he asked.

The skeleton nodded firmly. "I'll do whatever's needed to help Eddie," she said. Taking a deep breath, she lifted her skull from the top of her spine with a *click*, and handed it to Luke. The rest of the skeleton clattered to the ground, and

Eefa began to collect up the bones and lay them on the shop counter.

Luke dragged a chair over to the Horseman, climbed onto it and held the skull in place above his neck. "OK," he said. "It's demon-making time!"

Resus produced a toolbox from his cloak and handed it to Sir Otto, who then stepped up to the Horseman's body to begin attaching Femur's skull to the neck.

"I still don't understand why *he* has to do this," mumbled Cleo under her breath. "In the Underlands, we stitched a whole zombie back together ourselves."

"We need Sir Otto to repeat whatever he did when he built Ottostein," explained Luke. "It has to be exactly the same if we're going to stand any chance of defeating the original demon in a battle. Plus, I don't fancy trying my hand at connecting two different life-forms!"

Resus peered out of the shop window. Over at Sneer Hall, windows exploded as the demon hurled objects through them in rage. "We'd better get a move on," he sighed, "or Sir Otto will end up having to stay in our spare room as well!"

 99

Soon the task was completed. "That's it," said Sir Otto, standing back. "Now we just need to power it up." He eyed the bat, sleeping on its perch above the door.

"No way," warned Cleo. "You're not touching that bat!"

"Then we're in big trouble," grunted Sir Otto. "There's no way the head can send impulses to the body without an electrical charge."

Luke turned to Eefa. "Is there anything you can do?"

"I can try," said the witch. She stepped up to the figure and pointed a long, purple fingernail at the join between Femur's skull and Eddie's body, muttering the incantation she usually used to light candles. A single spark of power leapt from Eefa's finger and clung to the glue. The electricity spread, circling Eddie's neck again and again until he appeared to be wearing a blue, fizzing collar, just like Ottostein.

"What do you know," mumbled the landlord, sucking on his cigar. "It worked."

Cleo stuck her tongue out at him. "And without harming a single bat!"

"OK," said Luke, addressing Femur's skull.

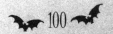

"The sword-fighting memories should still be in Eddie's muscles. All you have to do is dig deep and revive them."

Femur nodded and began to concentrate. Slowly, the Horseman's hand lifted, the silver sword glinting under the electric lights. Breathing deeply, Femur pictured Eddie heroically fighting off the giants who had attacked the orphanage, and silently she gave the order to fight. The Horseman's hand gripped the handle of his weapon, swung it around – and buried the blade deep into his own left thigh.

"It's in his leg!" squealed Rocky.

"It's OK," said Femur through gritted teeth, "I can take the pain."

"I'm not worried about *you*," barked the gargoyle. "Eddie's due to advertise his new range of underwear next week with that leg!

Cleo advanced on him, snarling. "If you don't shut up about Eddie's work commitments, I'll turn you into a garden decoration…" Rocky quickly closed his mouth and backed away into a corner.

"What's wrong?" Luke asked Femur. "Couldn't you find the muscle memories?"

"I found them OK," explained the skeleton,

"it's just that they seem to know absolutely nothing about sword-fighting."

"But Eddie said he'd saved an orphanage from rampaging giants…" began Resus.

Slowly, everybody in the emporium turned towards Rocky's cowering figure.

"How did the Horseman really lose his head?" Luke asked.

"I-it was like he s-said," stammered Rocky. "He was f-fighting giants…"

"I reckon you'd make a lovely water feature," said Cleo, advancing on the gargoyle.

"OK, OK!" squeaked Rocky. "Eddie doesn't know how to swordfight! He used to be an insurance clerk for G.H.O.U.L. and he lost his head a couple of years ago at an office party."

"How do you get your head chopped off at a party?" asked Resus incredulously.

Rocky looked as though he might be sick.

"He was photocopying his face for a bet when a shelf of phone directories fell on top of the photocopier lid and sliced his neck clean through. Luckily, there was a witch at the party who was able to keep him alive – so, we kept the head, bought him a horse and made the rest up."

Luke slumped into the chair recently vacated by the Horseman. "We're doomed," he groaned. "There's absolutely no way he can fight the demon."

Resus grinned and reached into his cloak. "Oh, I wouldn't say that…"

Luke took the wireless games controller from Resus. "Why are you carrying this around with you?" he asked.

"Now that you've got me into video games, I want to be ready when you fancy a rematch of Martial Arts Madness II!" beamed the vampire as he clamped the silver sword back into Eddie's hand. "Just let me know when you want your virtual butt kicked – I've been practising the moves, and I'm ready!"

"I've never really had a friend to play against before," said Luke.

Resus pulled a fearsome expression. "Friend-ship means nothing in the field of computerized combat!" Luke punched him playfully in the arm and grinned.

Femur's skull looked nervously at the remote gamepad. "So, I'll be out there, but you'll be controlling me from in here?" she asked.

Luke nodded. "It'll feel weird at first, but just relax and let me do the work."

Eefa took the gamepad from Luke and held it up so that the edge was touching the electric collar around the Horseman's neck. As she zapped the controller with her finger, it also crackled with power and glowed bright blue.

"OK," she said, handing it back to Luke. "Try that."

The controller vibrated with power in Luke's hands. Taking a deep breath, he pressed a button. The Headless Horseman's sword arm instantly raised up and then slashed down, hard. "Right," Luke murmured. "So, button A is a forehand attack…"

For the next few minutes, Luke practised controlling the Horseman's body, noting which combinations of buttons produced which moves.

 104

Before long, he could slash and stab with the sword, duck and dodge his opponent's attacks, and even head-butt with Femur's skull.

"Right," he said, turning to Resus. "Open the door. Let's go!"

Rocky stepped in front of the Horseman, blocking his exit. "That's it?" he asked. "You're just going to walk him out there?"

Cleo grabbed the broom again. "If you're going to cause trouble…"

Rocky held up his hands to placate her. "I might not know anything about fighting," he said, "but I do understand the most basic rule of show business." He smiled, flashing his pebble-like teeth. "Always make an entrance!"

Chapter Ten

The Battle

The doors to Everwell's Emporium crashed open and the figure made up of the Headless Horseman's body and Femur's skull rode out on Eddie's black stallion. Smoke billowed, and pounding music

– "Chomping Champion" by zombie rock band Brain Drain – blared out across the square.

"If I'd known you had stabled that horse in my storeroom…" growled Eefa.

"Shh," hissed Rocky. "You'll spoil the effect!"

"Well, you're cleaning it up!"

The doors slammed shut, cutting off the curtain of smoke. Inside the emporium, Cleo coughed. "You can put out those five extra cigars now," she said to Sir Otto. The landlord grumbled something about the expense, then disposed of the noxious stubs.

Resus switched off the CD player and slipped it back inside his cloak. "How are you doing?" he asked Luke.

"Fine, so far," replied Luke. He moved closer to the window and continued to press various different buttons on his glowing gamepad. "With any luck, we'll have the fifth relic in our hands before long."

Out in the square, the Horseman's collar sparked, causing his right hand to pull on the reins, turning the horse slightly. He rode over to the wall surrounding Sneer Hall and, following another command from Luke, rattled his sword across the spikes along the top.

After a few moments, Ottostein came bursting out of the mansion, his own collar fizzing.

"All right," said Luke. "Game on!"

The Headless Horseman's stallion retreated to the centre of the square and stood nervously as the demon stomped towards him across the gardens of Sneer Hall. Luke flicked a button that told the Horseman to run a hand comfortingly across its neck.

Ottostein crashed through the gates, causing Sir Otto to groan and cover his eyes.

"So," roared the demon, "they have created a

champion of their own. I relish the opportunity to crush you in battle!"

"It doesn't have to be like this," shouted the Horseman in Femur's voice. "Just return the skull, and the people of Scream Street can live their lives in peace."

"Peace is for cowards," bellowed the demon. "Heroes prefer conflict!"

Inside the emporium, Luke's fingers twitched as they hovered over the controls. "You want conflict," he muttered, "you've got it!" He pressed several buttons at once and the Horseman sprang into action, his electrical collar sparking with power. He flicked the reins and the stallion

galloped towards the monster. As the horse drew close, the Horseman raised his sword arm and slashed the blade down towards Ottostein.

The demon reacted quickly, snatching up a broken fencepost and blocking the blow. The Horseman struck again and Ottostein ducked beneath the blade before smacking its own weapon hard against the stallion's flank. The horse cried out and fell to the ground, dismounting its rider.

"That horse cost me thousands!" exclaimed Rocky as he pressed his stony face up against the glass. "But that's not the important thing right now," he added quickly as Resus clamped a hand down on his shoulder.

In the square, the stallion struggled to its feet before galloping away to safety. Luke ordered the Horseman back to his feet as Ottostein strode towards him. Femur's skull barely reached the monster's chest now that she was no longer in the saddle, but Luke did not let that distract him.

The Horseman suddenly dashed forward, smashing his sword down and burying the tip of the blade into the concrete. Using this as leverage, the Horseman flipped his body up and his feet connected hard with Ottostein's chin. More of the glue separated around the creature's neck, and it staggered backwards from the blow.

Resus gazed at Luke in admiration. "The ultimate move from Martial Arts Madness II," he grinned. "Looks like I'll have my work cut out beating you after all!"

Luke allowed himself a brief smile, then focused back on the controls. The Horseman wrenched his sword from the ground and swung it round in a low arc. Ottostein went to lift its powerful centaur's limb out of the way, but it was too late and the blade cut into its leg, slicing off the ankle. Everyone in the emporium winced as the detached hoof bounced across the square.

"Stay focused," said Luke to himself as Ottostein crashed to the ground. He didn't want to stop now he finally had the advantage. As the demon flipped onto its back, Rocky noticed that one of Eddie's horns had snapped off and gave an involuntary groan.

Ordering the Horseman to stand over the defeated demon, Luke lifted his sword hand high in the air. The blade glinted in the sunlight as he pressed the button to strike. Nothing happened.

Out in the square, Femur stared down at Ottostein. "I don't want to do this," she said, using all her effort to keep the Horseman's hand from striking. "I don't want to hurt you."

Inside the emporium, Luke pressed repeatedly at the attack button. "What's wrong?" demanded Sir Otto, rubbing his bloodshot eyes. "Why aren't you killing it?"

"I'm trying," said Luke, "but the attack command won't work!"

"It's Femur," said Cleo with pride. "She's blocking the signal. She's giving the demon a chance to do the right thing!"

Ottostein glared up at its opponent with flashing eyes as Femur spoke again. "All you have to do is end the violence, and we can find a way to replace the Horseman's head with one of your own." The demon's lights dimmed briefly and, for a brief second, Femur saw a glint of Eddie's blue eyes behind the green.

"You could live with us in Scream Street," Femur insisted. "We could arrange with G.H.O.U.L. to find you a—"

Suddenly, the demon hurled its fencepost like a spear, the jagged point lodging into the join

between the Horseman's body and Femur's skull. The electrical collar flashed and died as the body crumpled to the ground.

"No!" screeched Luke, hammering at the gamepad. The blue power fizzed for a second, then the light went out. "I've lost control!"

Outside, the Horseman's body twitched involuntarily on the concrete before lying still.

"We've got to save Femur," shouted Cleo, wrenching open the shop door and racing outside.

"Cleo, come back!" ordered Eefa. But the mummy ignored her and carried on running as the demon clambered to its remaining hooves and lifted the Horseman into the air. Roaring triumphantly, Ottostein hung the lifeless body on top of one of the few sections of wall around Sneer Hall that was still standing.

"I knew this would all end in tears," growled Sir Otto.

"That's it!" cried Luke. "Of course!" He rushed for the shop doorway. "Resus, I'm going to need two halves of an onion…"

"I'm on it!" called the vampire, thrusting his hands deep into his cloak as Luke dashed outside.

Ottostein grinned crazily as it watched Cleo run to the Horseman's aid. Femur's skull sobbed as it hung on the metal spike, held there by the weight of the body. "Now," bellowed the demon, "I shall crush you all!" Its collar sparked and fizzed as it limped towards them.

Standing at the doors to the emporium, Resus finally found an onion in the folds of his cloak and produced a knife shortly after. "Luke," he yelled as he threw the two halves across the square. "Incoming!"

Luke turned just long enough to catch the onion halves, then continued running towards the monster. "Cleo!" he called. "Get down!"

Cleo dropped to her hands and knees just in time and Luke planted a foot on her back, launching himself towards the approaching demon. Gripping Ottostein's one remaining horn, he rammed the onion halves deep into Eddie's eye sockets.

Immediately, the extra tear ducts Eddie had had fitted sprang to life, sending tears pouring down the Horseman's skull. Luke jumped free of the snarling creature just as the torrent reached the demon's electrical collar. There was a flash of blue light and Ottostein's head erupted into flames as the liberal application of Decapitation Pour L'Homme coating the skull was ignited.

"No!" squealed Rocky as he watched his source of income go up in smoke. He burst out of the emporium and dashed across the square, granite wings flapping.

Ottostein roared in pain, frantically batting at its head to try to put out the flames. In a last-gasp effort to save itself before the fire spread to its body, the demon reached up with its powerful minotaur arm, gripped Eddie's skull and tore it away from its body. With the electrical connection now severed, the fire flickered out just as the demon's body collapsed to the ground.

Rocky leapt forward to save Eddie's head, only to be flattened with a *crunch* as the demon's lifeless body fell on top of him. The skull bounced on the concrete and Luke raised his hand to catch it bowling-ball style — with two fingers up its nostrils and his thumb in its mouth.

After a moment's silence, Resus punched his fist into the air and whooped with joy. "Now *that*," he grinned, "is how you get a*head*!"

Chapter Eleven
The Truth

Luke was busy

scraping soot from the Headless Horseman's head as Cleo and Eefa carried Femur's skeleton out of the emporium and laid it on the ground in the square. "I hope the magic still works after a relic has been barbecued," he laughed.

Cleo retrieved Femur's skull from near the Horseman's body. "Are you OK?"

116

"I'll be fine," Femur assured her. "I'm just happy no one else was hurt."

"You're an inspiration," sighed Cleo. "Not many people would have given the demon a chance to live in Scream Street after all that destruction."

Luke stopped scraping and looked at Cleo thoughtfully. "You're right," he said. Setting the Horseman's head aside, he pulled *Skipstone's Tales of Scream Street* from his pocket and addressed the author. "Eddie's skull isn't the one I need, is it."

Samuel Skipstone opened his eyes. "I never said it was."

"I know," said Luke. "You said I was searching for *a skull unlike the rest*. That had nothing to do with horns and fangs, did it? It was to do with its owner."

"I don't get it," admitted Cleo.

"Think about it," said Luke. "Femur was strong enough to control the Horseman's body, yet Eddie was powerless when connected to the demon."

"So?" said Resus. "You mean she's some kind of skeleton superhero?"

"Even better," answered Luke, turning to Femur just as Eefa reattached her skull to her

spine. "You're one of the founding fathers, aren't you. Or do I call you a founding mother?"

"The choice is yours," smiled Femur. "But now you'll be needing to take my skull to complete this section of your quest."

Luke glanced down at the Headless Horseman's head on the ground beside him. "Not just yet…"

Femur raised her wine glass and stared deep into Eddie's blue eyes. The Horseman, his head still blackened from the fire and one horn glued back on somewhat wonkily, smiled at her. "To us," he said, clinking his own glass against hers.

The pair were sitting at a table set up in the centre of the square, enjoying a candlelit meal while the residents of Scream Street set about repairing their homes.

A few jealous females flashed envious scowls at Femur, but the lovestruck skeleton didn't notice. "I'm glad your eyes are back to their original colour," she said. "Green just didn't suit you."

The Horseman ran his hand over his cracked and blistered skull. "It can't be pleasant for you, looking at this mess," he said.

"It makes no difference to me," said Femur truthfully.

"Even now you know I made up the whole story about the orphanages?" asked Eddie. "Even now you know I'm not a hero?"

"I spent long enough connected to your body to know that you're a hero inside," she replied. "Plus, you've *had* a real battle now – here in Scream Street."

"It's not the same, though, is it?" said Eddie. "I let all my fans down by lying to them. They'll never look at me in the same way again."

"They will if we make sure they never hear the truth," grinned Femur.

Across the table, the Headless Horseman took

her hand in his. "Luke was right," he said. "You really *are* special!"

Cleo watched the couple from her position on the pavement outside Everwell's Emporium. "This has been the most romantic Halloween in years," she cooed.

"I hope you feel the same way after I've thrown up everywhere," grumbled Resus. "This is way off the top of the mushometer!"

"Will you watch what you're doing?" snarled a gravelly voice beside him. "You've just glued my ear to my forehead!"

Resus paused in his task and studied his handiwork. "There's still time for me to turn you into that fountain for Cleo's garden, you know," he said to the ungrateful gargoyle. "Remember that I'm rebuilding you out of the goodness of my heart!"

The vampire had already reattached Doug's arm with the strong glue, and the zombie was now rotating his shoulder to test the result. "Better than ever, little dude!" he beamed.

The bat screeched as the door to Everwell's Emporium opened and Luke emerged carrying a bottle filled with yellow liquid. "Eefa charged this to Sir Otto's account," he said, handing it to Doug. "Think of it as his way of saying sorry for chopping your arm off."

Doug read the label on the bottle. "Freshly squeezed bile!" he exclaimed. "Mucho gratitude, dude. Turf and Berry are cooking a nice, juicy spleen for supper and this will complement it nicely!" And with that the zombie lurched away happily, glad to be back in one piece.

"A spleen for supper?" groaned Cleo. "I think I might throw up too."

"Well, you can give me a hand with this before you do," said Luke. The disassembled parts of Ottostein lay beside him on the ground and needed to go back into their original Oddbods crates. Each box now bore a sticker that read "Return to sender".

"That's it!" snapped Rocky, glaring at Resus. "I'm sure you just glued all my fingers onto one hand on purpose. I went out of my way to help you stop that demon, and I deserve to be treated with a little *mmph-mpph-mm-mmm*!"

"Oh dear," exclaimed Resus in mock surprise. "I appear to have accidentally glued Rocky's mouth closed…"

Back at the table, the Horseman stood. "I'm afraid I must go," he said to Femur. "I'm due at a book-signing in Atlantis tonight, and I can't let my fans down!"

"Thank you," the skeleton sighed. "This has been wonderful."

"No," said Eddie. "*You've* been wonderful."

Femur closed her eyes as the Headless Horseman bent to kiss her, but nothing happened. Opening them again, she saw to her horror that Eddie's head was missing once again. A foul stench of cigars filled the air. The skeleton gasped.

"The rest of you might be travelling by Hex Hatch," Sir Otto growled to the Horseman, "but I'll be keeping the head for myself!"

Luke paused from dropping the damaged centaur's leg into a crate and ran over. "We had a deal," he insisted. "You said you'd help us stop the demon and get the head back!"

"Which is exactly what I did," grinned Sir Otto. "But I like to think I've moved on from there." He held the Horseman's head up to the light to examine it. "Now I have my first relic, and it won't be long until—"

A black-gloved hand grabbed his ear tightly.

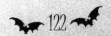

"Dixon!" barked Queenie Sneer. "Take that head from your pathetic uncle and give it back to its rightful owner. Even *I've* worked out that it's not one of the precious relics."

"Right away, Mummy," squeaked Dixon, sticking his tongue out at the crestfallen Sir Otto as he snatched the skull from his hands and passed it back to the grateful Horseman.

"If there's one thing I enjoy more than annoying the freaks," snarled Queenie, "it's bullying my baby brother!" She gave Sir Otto's ear a painful twist before finally releasing it. "What a dump," she added, gazing around Scream Street.

"Well," said the Horseman, "if you're looking to get out of here, I've got an opening for a new agent. Rocky's in no shape to come with me, and someone with your bullying abilities could become really quite successful at it."

Queenie's eyes flickered with interest. "There's bullying involved?"

The Headless Horseman nodded. "Plus a fair amount of intimidation, threat-making and plain, old-fashioned name-calling. G.H.O.U.L. should be opening a Hex Hatch for me at any moment."

"Where do I sign?" smiled Queenie, cracking her knuckles.

The Horseman raised his fingers to his mouth and whistled. His jet-black stallion galloped over and stopped at his side. As Eddie swung himself into the saddle, pulling Queenie up behind him, the air in the centre of the square began to shimmer.

"This is to say thank you!" he called, tossing something to Cleo. Then, with a wink at Femur, he rode the horse straight towards the Hex Hatch. Leaping high, the Headless Horseman and Queenie Sneer disappeared from sight.

"What did he give you?" asked Luke.

Cleo opened her hand to reveal a tiny perfume bottle with a miniature skull on top. "Decapitation Pour L'Homme!" she giggled, pinching her nose.

"Ooh," said Dixon, nudging his uncle. "I've heard that's really nice. Maybe you should get some too, Otto."

"*Otto?*" roared the landlord. "OTTO?" He turned on Dixon, his face purple. "And don't think I've forgotten your behaviour over the past twenty-four hours…"

Dixon began to back away towards Sneer Hall as the furious landlord gave chase. "I'm sorry, Sir Uncle Otto," he squeaked.

"At least some things are getting back to normal round here," grinned Resus.

"Are you sure you're going to be OK in there?" asked Luke as he lowered Femur's skull into the golden casket that Cleo had given him to store the relics in. Already in there were a vampire's fang, a vial of witch's blood, the heart of an ancient mummy and a zombie's tongue.

"I'll be fine," replied Femur. "And I'll have Samuel for company."

"Indeed you shall," agreed the face on the cover of *Skipstone's Tales of Scream Street*. "We go back a long way, Femur and I." The author looked up at Luke. "How are your parents?"

"Recovering," replied Luke. "We'll be staying with Resus's mum and dad while we fix the house up." He gestured towards the remains of the staircase outside his bedroom. "I never thought I'd be sorry to see this place get damaged."

"This is your home," said Skipstone. "At least for the moment. You are but one relic away from possessing the powers of the founding fathers, Luke Watson. Then you will have the ability to return to your previous life."

Luke sighed heavily. "I know."

"Is there a problem?" enquired the author. "I thought you were keen to leave Scream Street behind and go back to your own world?"

Luke gazed out of his broken bedroom window at the twisted, misshapen houses across the street. "So did I, Mr Skipstone," he said. "So did I."

Tommy Donbavand was born and brought up in Liverpool and has worked at numerous careers that have included clown, actor, theatre producer, children's entertainer, drama teacher, storyteller and writer. His non-fiction books for children and their parents, *Boredom Busters* and *Quick Fixes for Bored Kids*, have helped him to become a regular guest on radio stations around the UK and he also writes for a number of magazines, including *Creative Steps* and Scholastic's *Junior Education*.

Tommy sees his new comedy-horror series as what might have resulted had Stephen King been the author of *Scooby Doo*. "Writing *Scream Street* is fangtastic fun," he says. "I just have to be careful not to scare myself too much!" Tommy lives in Lancashire with his family and sees sleep as a waste of good writing time.

You can find out more about Tommy and his books at his website: www.tommydonbavand.com